SPECIAL CROSSOVER EDITION

HORSE DIARIES
·Cinders·

HORSE DIARIES

SPECIAL CROSSOVER EDITION

HORSE DIARIES

Cinders

KATE KLIMO

illustrated by RUTH SANDERSON

RANDOM HOUSE NEW YORK

The author and editor would like to thank Russell Lewis,
executive vice president and chief historian at Chicago History Museum,
for his assistance in the preparation of this book.

Visit us on the Web! randomhousekids.com

Educators and librarians, for a variety of teaching tools, visit us at
RHTeachersLibrarians.com

Library of Congress Cataloging-in-Publication Data
Names: Klimo, Kate. | Sanderson, Ruth, illustrator.
Title: Cinders / Kate Klimo ; illustrated by Ruth Sanderson.
Description: First edition. | New York : Random House, [2016] |
Series: Horse diaries, special edition | Summary: "Cinders is a dappled gray
Percheron horse during the 1871 Great Chicago Fire" —Provided by publisher. |
Includes bibliographical references.
Identifiers: LCCN 2015020129 | ISBN 978-1-101-93690-0 (trade pbk.) |
ISBN 978-1-101-93691-7 (lib. bdg.) | ISBN 978-1-101-93692-4 (ebook)
Subjects: LCSH: Percheron horse—Juvenile fiction. | CYAC: Percheron horse—
Fiction. | Horses—Fiction. | Great Fire, Chicago, Ill., 1871—Fiction.
Classification: LCC PZ10.3.K686 Ci 2016 | DDC [Fic]—dc23

Printed in the United States of America
10 9 8 7 6 5 4 3 2 1
First Edition

For Karen Kolster,
the best barn-buddy ever

—K.K.

In memory of Paul Moshimer

—R.S.

CONTENTS

"Oh! if people knew what a comfort to horses a light hand is . . ."
—from *Black Beauty,* by Anna Sewell

SPECIAL CROSSOVER EDITION

HORSE DIARIES

Cinders

LITTLE GIANT No. 6, 1874

There really was a fire station on Maxwell Street. It was the home of the Little Giant, among the city's first steam engines and the first rig to show up at the scene of the Great Fire. The characters in this story—dog, horse, and human—are figments of this author's imagination.

1865: DeKalb, Illinois

The Little Ones named me. Although I was born black, they were betting that my coat and mane would soon turn as silvery-gray as my dam's. Sure enough, they did. And so I was called Cinders. My earliest memories are of the Little Ones slipping between the fence boards into our paddock.

Under Mother's watchful eye, they brushed out my coat and kissed my nose and draped me in garlands woven from prairie flowers.

When I nibbled at the sweet blossoms, they scolded me.

Farmer Zeke said, "Abigail, Trudy, remember that Cinders is a Percheron. She's going to grow up to be a big, strong farm horse, not some fancy lady's mount."

The Little Ones sighed. "Oh, Papa! We know that! But she'll always be our doll baby!"

No sooner had Mother returned to work in the field than I began following the Little Ones almost everywhere a growing filly could go.

When Abigail fed the chickens, I carried the feed sack across my back. Newly hatched, the puffs of yellow down scurried around my feet

and I had to pick my way through them with the greatest care.

When Trudy entered the garden to flick the bugs off the leaves, I followed her up and down the rows without treading on a single plant.

When the Little Ones collected the eggs, I waited for them outside the henhouse. One time, they balanced a row of eggs in the hollow of my back. I bore my fragile cargo all the way to the back door.

The girls, dancing around me and clapping their hands, cried out, "Mama! Come see!"

Mrs. Zeke came out onto the porch. "You gals try hard enough and you'll spoil that horse for *real* work."

By the time the snow was deep, the Little Ones were clambering onto my back from the porch rail. On their own two feet, they sank into the drifts up to their middles. But I held them above it all. A kick of the boot heel or a tug of my mane was all the guidance I needed.

Sometimes they put a rope around my neck and hitched me to an old blanket. I would drag them around on top of the snow.

Such was my life—and a finer one no horse could have asked for. Then, in my third spring, Farmer Zeke came to the paddock with a rope and a halter and I sensed change in the air.

I walked up and leaned into him the way I did when I was hankering for a hug.

One hand planted firmly on my nose, he pushed me away. "You've got your space and I've got mine," he said. "You don't come into mine unless I invite you."

I pulled back and licked my lips. The look in his eyes told me I must watch and listen and keep my distance until I was asked to come closer.

He slipped the halter over my head, and I followed him meekly to the pen outside the barn.

The Little Ones perched on the rail. "Can we watch you work with Cinders, Papa?" they asked.

"Nope. If you're here, she'll spend all her time making goo-goo eyes at you and she won't listen to a thing I say."

The Little Ones dropped down and went away.

Farmer Zeke took an empty feed sack and flapped it at me. I pulled back. I was used to playing games with the Little Ones, but this was new to me.

Then he held the bag out to me. I thrust my head forward and sniffed. I smelled old corn. I blew out. He took the bag and rubbed it over my ears and around my mouth and between my legs and even under my tail.

Then he got a blanket and a leather thing and, one after the other, put them under my nose to sniff. I blew out again. They smelled like horse sweat.

"This is a blanket and a saddle, Cinders."

He put the blanket, then the saddle, on my back, and fastened a strap beneath my belly. My blood boiled and my skin seethed. I tried to heave the saddle over my shoulders. When that didn't work, I ran around trying to buck it off. Then I got down on the ground and tried to roll it away.

Farmer Zeke stood in the middle of the pen and watched me with calm eyes. I carried on until I was all worn out. Then I went to the edge of the pen. I dropped my head and lost myself in the grass. Soon I forgot the saddle was even there. It never bothered me again.

In the days that followed, I got used to Farmer Zeke digging around in my hooves with a pick. I learned that whenever his hands touched my knee, I was meant to bend my leg and offer him my hoof.

Another day, he put a hand on my shoulder. His hand pressed into me, harder and harder. Finally, I picked up my hoof and moved away from the pressure. He took his hand away and then patted me. He did the same thing with all four of my legs. After a while, it got so that I could move every which way at a featherlight touch.

Next, he attached a longer rope to my halter. He stood a ways off and touched my haunch with a stick and said, "Go!"

I moved around him at the end of the rope. When he placed himself on the other side of my nose, I knew he wanted me to turn and go the other way. This was not new to me. Pointing with her nose, this was how Mother moved me around the paddock. After I had learned to go in both directions at a walk, he drove me into a trot, a canter, and a gallop.

As for the hard bar, that was no fun at all! The only reason I let him put it in my mouth was that it tasted like molasses. But when I had licked off all the sweetness, I was left with the cold taste of metal. It made my mouth water and my tongue slurp.

The *bit*, he called it. It was attached to two leather lines he called *reins*. When Zeke tugged on the reins, the bar bit into the sides of my mouth.

It was a few days later when Farmer Zeke put

the bit in my mouth and attached a long rope to each side of it. He laid the ropes behind me and went to stand between them some distance behind my tail. I turned and whickered, *What are you up to now?*

"You need to get used to my being behind you like this, Cinders."

I snorted. This was how Mother sometimes used to herd me, with her nose to my tail. I sighed and smacked my lips, then turned and faced front. I felt him lift the ropes. He sent a gentle wave through the ropes that reached the bit. "Walk on!" he said.

I started moving. We walked around the pen. His hands spoke through the ropes and told me what he wanted. "Walk on." "Turn this way." "Turn that way." "Trot." "Back up." "Whoa."

Then one fine day he put me in harness

and attached me to the wagon. The Little Ones spilled out of the house and climbed up into the seat with their father.

Farmer Zeke picked up the reins and said, "Walk on," and I jogged around the pen in a circle, pulling the wagon. After a few more turns, my heart leaped when Farmer Zeke guided me out the gate and down the barn lane.

I shook my mane and snorted with pleasure as I broke into a brisk trot. This was the job that I was put on earth to do.

1868: Dark Days

That winter, the snow lay deep upon the ground. Day after day, Mother and I stood idle in the paddock.

Farmer Zeke came out twice a day to put down hay. Then he turned around and trudged back to the house. Sometimes a Little One would press her nose to the window and stare at us with the saddest eyes.

Come and play! I called to her.

But she shook her head and ducked out of sight.

Something is not right, Mother said.

Then one day, Farmer Zeke came and led Mother away. I tried to follow, but he blocked me with a hand.

"You've never pulled a sled before, and this is not the time to train you," he said.

I watched as he hitched Mother up to the wagon, whose wheels had been replaced by two sharp metal blades. This, then, was what he called a sled. He took a seat and lifted the reins. With a smooth *whoosh* of its blades, the sled disappeared over the rise.

Some time later, the sled returned carrying a

stranger in a black coat. Swinging a black bag, he hurried after Farmer Zeke into the house.

Mother waited out front, still in harness. She stomped and snorted, her breath smoky in the cold air. I could tell from her heaving sides and her sweat-darkened coat that she had run a long distance in a short time.

She called out to me, *Something is terribly wrong!*

I called back to her, *You're frightening me, Mother!*

It wasn't long before the stranger came out with Farmer Zeke. The stranger put a hand on Zeke's arm. Zeke bowed his head. From inside the house, I could hear the two Little Ones keening. I paced along the fence line until I had worried a deep muddy groove in the snow.

After that, people came to the house. They arrived in sleds, on horseback, and on snowshoes. With sad faces, they entered the house carrying dishes of food. The house echoed with the sound of their voices. At long last, the back door opened and the Little Ones burst out.

I tossed my mane. I was ready to play and learn new tricks! After climbing the fence, they threw their arms around me and burst into tears.

"Mama is with the angels!" Abigail cried.

"And we're going back East to live with Grandmama," Trudy sobbed.

"We're selling the farm and all the equipment and stock—including you!" Abigail gasped.

"We begged Papa to let us take you, but he told us you'd be miserable on the noisy, dirty streets of New York City," Trudy bawled.

I didn't understand. Why were the Little Ones so sad?

As the snow thawed, more people came to the farm. They walked around and chatted with Farmer Zeke and left with pieces of his equipment. One man took a plow. Another took some hoes. Yet another took Mother away, hitched to the back of his wagon. Now *I* was sad!

I followed her along the fence line until I could go no farther, calling out, *Take me with you, Mother!*

Farewell, Cinders, she called back. *Just be your good, sweet self and everyone will love you.*

I moped in the paddock. Many people wanted to take me away. Finally, I was sold to Old Man Muller for what Farmer Zeke called "a tidy sum."

The Little Ones stomped their feet.

"How *could* you, Papa?" said Trudy.

"Mr. Muller is one of the hardest-working farmers in these parts," said Farmer Zeke.

"He's mean as *spit* and everybody knows it," said Abigail.

"He'll whip our darling Cinders!" said Trudy.

"Now, girls, that's not being very Christian about your neighbor," said Farmer Zeke.

"He'll be mean to our doll baby!" said Abigail.

"Your *doll baby* is fifteen hands high and will grow to be seventeen hands," said Farmer Zeke. "I think she can take care of herself."

That last day, the girls clung to me and soaked my mane with their tears. They draped a garland of prairie flowers around my neck. Then I watched as they drove away in a wagon loaded up with all their worldly goods . . . except for me.

* * *

Old Man Muller worked his horse like he worked his land and his sons: hard and long and without mercy.

In the early summer, I pulled the harrow so that the old man could get his seeds in. When the grass grew high, I dragged the mower to cut it. Later, I pulled the wagon through the fields and stood while the sons jumped out and bundled the grass into shocks and tossed them into the back.

In the late summer, the sons toiled at either end of a long, sharp, jagged blade. They sawed down a whole forest of trees. "Timber!" they shouted as the trees came crashing down.

After all the trees were down, the old man hitched the logs to my harness. I dragged them off to a big pile.

Then the sons went through and picked out the stones and boulders, which I hauled away on a sled. After many days of sawing and hauling, the field was clear except for the tree stumps.

The son called Junior said, "There's only one way to get them stumps out, Daddy, and that's good old-fashioned elbow grease."

The one called Bud shook his head. "Digging them up is way too much work. Get me enough gunpowder and I'll blast them out for you, Pops. *Boom!*" He laughed and slapped his knee.

I remembered the *booms* Bud made. When I first heard them, I thought the sky was falling. I ran from one end of the paddock to the other, looking for somewhere to hide. But after I had heard them enough times, I stopped spooking. I knew the noise was just Bud blowing something up.

"Don't need elbow grease or gunpowder," the old man growled. "We got us Cinders." He smacked me on the haunch, and I jumped in my skin.

I should have been used to his ways by now. The old man never petted unless he could smack, never spoke unless he could yell, never asked nicely if he could demand.

"This horse here," he said with another stinging slap, "could move a mountain if we hitched her up to it and whupped her hard enough!"

They tied one end of a chain to the tree stump and the other to my harness. The old man got behind me and grabbed the reins. "Pull!"

I pulled as hard as I could, but I was going nowhere except deeper into the earth up to my fetlocks.

"Pull!" he roared, and he lay into me with the whip.

I strained against the harness. He lashed me again and again. Streams of sweat ran down my sides. I pulled until I thought my heart would burst. I felt the roots begin to loosen their grip,

one by one. He kept after me with the whip. Then came the loud ripping sound as the last roots gave way. I lunged forward, dragging the tree stump behind me.

The sons cheered. Then, without pausing to let me rest, they urged me on to the next tree

stump. By the time the stumps were all cleared, my body was so sore I hobbled back to the paddock. The sons rubbed me down.

When I was fit to go back to work, I pulled the wagon through the fields while the men loaded up the harvest to take to market.

On market day, the air was biting cold, and the sky hung as low and damp as a blanket on a swaybacked mule. There was already snow on the ground, so they hitched me up to the sleigh. And it was a good thing they did, because by the time we got to the city, big flakes of snow were drifting down.

In the marketplace, everyone was nervous, eager to finish business before the snow got too deep. But the old man took his time. "I ain't afraid of no snow," he muttered.

1869: Man-Killer!

The snow hardened and pelted down. It blew into my eyes and buried the road. I felt my way along.

The old man kept yanking me off course. In time, I grew weary of him scoring my back with the whip and sawing at my mouth with the bit. I gave in and let him lead.

By nightfall we came to a fork in the road. I had no idea which route to take, and neither did Old Man Muller. He hauled back on the reins. I stopped.

He said, "Stupid mare! Don't you even know the way home?" He snapped the whip at my head.

I flicked one ear, but that was all I intended to move. I knew that no matter which road I chose, we would be more lost than ever.

Ignoring his curses and the sting of the whip, I pulled the sled around. If I moved quickly, I might be able to find my way back to the place where the old man had yanked me off course in the first place.

"You'd better know what you're doing, horse!" he grumbled.

With a weary groan, he set aside the whip and

tied the reins to the dashboard. Then he wrapped his coat around himself and hunkered down. "Take me home, Cinders, before these old bones of mine freeze."

These were the last words I would ever hear him say.

Given my head, I broke into a trot, my hooves punching holes in the snow. It was hard going, but I didn't dare let up.

I kept up my pace even when it got colder and the snow turned to icy shards. It stung my eyes and coated my hide. The hard crust of ice on top of the snow cut into my legs. The harness rubbed my wet skin raw.

In the early hours, the storm passed. Although my leg muscles stung with weariness, I began to run. I sensed home nearby.

I ran until light glimmered low in the sky and I passed through the familiar gates. The sons had shoveled the barn road, and the surface was as slick as soap. Up ahead, the windows of the house glowed.

Mrs. Muller ran out onto the porch, waving her arms. Suddenly, the old man stirred to life. He heaved himself to his feet. At first I thought he was waving back to her. Then his face darkened and he gasped. He clutched his chest, wheezed, and pitched forward over the dashboard.

I froze in my tracks.

Mrs. Muller screamed and came running, followed by the sons, slipping and sliding across the ice.

Junior skidded to a stop and grabbed my nose-band. "Move off my old man!" he shouted.

"Move, you dumb mare!" Bud slammed me in the shoulder with a shovel blade.

I slewed to one side. And that's when I felt a crunch beneath my foot.

From the way they were all carrying on, I knew I had done something terrible. But had I really? I alone knew that the old man was already dead when he hit the ground. But since my hoof marked his head, they blamed his death on me.

Unbrushed, unfed, unwatered, I stood in harness all morning while people swarmed over the front yard. First, they carted off the body. Then they called in the doctor. All the while, Mrs. Muller wept and moaned. Later, people stood around and argued.

"If we sell her quick, we can still get a good price," Junior said.

"Too late," a friend said. "Word's already out. Everybody knows you got a man-killer on your hands."

"Man-killer, eh?" said Bud. "Well, ain't that just fine and dandy!"

I hung my head in shame. I was no longer Cinders. I was Man-Killer. Whatever it meant, I felt the name sear itself into me like a brand.

"You best save yourself the trouble and put her down right now," the friend said. "It's the only thing to do with a horse that's gone bad."

I knew that word: *bad*. Had I gone bad, like moldy hay or a wormy apple? I had always been good. Where was the sweet horse Mother had loved? Where was the doll baby the Little Ones had strewn with garlands? Or the steadfast farm worker?

They unhitched me from the wagon and left me tethered to a tree. Still no brush, no feed, no water. I stood around and shivered. The whip sores on my back stung.

Some time later, a man I did not know came and, with nervous hands, untied me and yanked me toward the barn.

I had always been an outdoor horse, even on the harshest winter days. Muller's barn was big and dark and musty and terrifying.

"Get into that stall, Man-Killer!"

The man shouted and waved his arms, but I planted my feet and set my teeth and refused to move.

He took up a pitchfork.

Old Man Muller had been a hard man, but he had never meant me ill. I reared.

"Get in there!" He lunged at me and caught me in the ribs with the pitchfork.

Screaming, I wheeled around and fled into a wooden box filled with straw. He slammed the door shut and walked away.

I felt the walls close in on me. I paced and tried to kick my way out. Finally, I gave up.

People came to visit me.

"That's the Man-Killer."

"She's got a murderous gleam in her eye, she does."

A little boy poked a sharp stick through the bars. "Come and get me, Killer," he said.

I shrank to the back of the stall.

I remained there for days on end. No one tended to my wounds. No one cleaned the stall.

I stood in the dirty straw and dung and urine. The only time I saw a human face was when a son came to shove stale hay through the bars or top off the water in the bucket.

One night Bud banged in, smelling of strong spirits and carrying a gun. I had seen him with the gun, blasting birds and rabbits in the fields. Trapped in the stall, I was easy prey.

He rested the barrel on the sill and aimed it between my eyes. He slid back the hammer.

I fixed him with a pleading look.

His hand on the trigger trembled.

I broke out in a sweat. My chest heaved. I began to wheeze.

In the end, he shook his head and lowered the gun. "I can't do it," he said. "You didn't kill my old man. It was my own fault. I was in such a rush to get the old man out from underfoot, I forced you to trample him."

That night, Bud went away and never came back.

Junior took care of me now. But there were days when he stayed away. One morning he arrived with something behind his back. I feared for my life. Then I saw that it was just a halter and lead rope!

When he slid open the door, I stepped forward and dropped my head so he could slip the halter on. Following him out of the barn, I stepped into dazzling sunlight.

The sap had risen. The buds had sprouted. The birds were chirping. While I had been locked away in the barn, spring had arrived. Was I going to the paddock now? My heart leaped. I would drink from the pond and graze until my belly ached, and then I would go down on my knees and roll in the sweet prairie flowers.

Instead, he led me to a place out beyond the barn, past the old pigsty, to a small fenced-in spot where the Muller family tossed their trash.

So I was trash now, was I?

There, I spent my days among the old rigs and rusting barrels. I picked my way through the broken glass and rusty wire in search of a few pale blades of grass. And when the grass was all gone, I licked the rotten timbers crawling with maggots.

I was dizzy from hunger and thirst. My ribs poked out. My hooves had grown so long that I wobbled when I walked.

When the stranger showed up one day, my

only thought was, *Another one out to get the Man-Killer, eh? Well, I'll give him something to fear!*

I reared, my hooves crashing into the fence post until it splintered. Then I tore around, fire flashing in my eyes, steam chuffing from my nostrils, wind ripping my mane.

Come and get me if you dare!

He stood and watched me with calm eyes, arms hanging at his sides.

Suddenly, all my rage and fear drained away like water from a rusty bucket. I came to a stop not far from him. Dropping my head, I heaved a sigh of pure weariness.

The man pushed his hat back. "So you're done with your little temper tantrum, are you now, Cinders?"

My ears twitched. He had a gentle voice. I lifted my head. He had a kind face. I licked my dry lips and chewed.

"Man-Killer, huh?" he said.

I blew out and shook my mane.

"I didn't think so. Although if I were you, I'd

hunt down the son of a gun who put me in here and give him a swift kick in the britches."

I walked up to him. He reached over the rail and stroked my neck.

"You've had a rough time of it, haven't you, girl?"

I pushed my nose into his hand and licked the salt off his palm.

"I'll tell you what, Cinders," he said, offering me the other hand. "I don't know you from Adam, and for all I know you've got a mean streak a mile and a half wide. But I'm of the opinion that everyone deserves a second chance."

Summer 1870: Downers Grove

When days passed and he didn't return, my hopes faded. It was just a matter of time, I believed, before the Knackers came to claim me.

Mother had told me about the Knackers. They were the men who came for horses when they were too worn out to work. They were dragged away to a Terrible Place and never seen or heard from again.

I knew I was too weak and tired to work. That's why when the three boys showed up in a wagon one morning, I took them for the Knackers.

If they wanted to haul me away to the Terrible Place, I was not going without a fight.

For an exhausted, starved horse, I pitched one ripsnorter of a battle. I kicked and squealed like a stuck pig. I lowered my head and charged them like an angry bull. Whenever I came within reach of the loops of their flying ropes, I reared, then wheeled and ran.

Those boys were cut and bruised and bleeding by the time they backed me into a corner and got the first loop over my head. By the time they had secured the third, I was all done in. They swung on the ropes and pulled me to my knees. I collapsed in a sweating heap.

I give up, I wheezed.

For a few moments, they bent over with their elbows on their knees, catching their breath. They glared at me, daring me to start up again.

"Finn is gonna be mighty sorry he ever rescued her," said one.

"Let's get her to the farm before she gets a second wind," said another.

"She may rally and kill us yet," said the third.

I let them pull me to my feet and lead me out. They put a halter and a lead rope on me and, one by one, warily slipped off the loops. Then they tied me to the back of the wagon.

One of the two draft horses pulling the wagon

turned around and gave me a look. She nickered, *What were you trying to prove?*

They're taking me to the Knackers, I said. *I won't go meekly.*

Her teammate tossed back her head and whinnied with mirth. *Is that what you thought? Well, you're in for a big surprise.*

We traveled for some time, me keeping pace with the team and eating their dust. In the early afternoon, we arrived in a valley smelling of new-mown hay.

Around a big house attached to an even bigger barn, a sorry-looking assortment of goats, roosters, ducks, donkeys, cats, and dogs wandered free as you please. In a vast, rolling pasture, a herd of swaybacked Percherons grazed.

The man who had found me in the Mullers'

junkyard was waiting next to a grassy pen with a stream running through it.

"Welcome to Second Chance Farm, Cinders," the man said.

The boys unhitched me.

One said, "She's a mean cuss, Mister Finn."

"Well, maybe she'll settle down once she sees she's among friends." Finn rested a hand on my nose. "I bet you thought I'd forgotten you. Well, we had to get the hay in before I could spare the boys. From the looks of them, you put up a good fight."

They put me in the pen.

"Better hobble her in case she decides to get frisky," Finn said. "I'd hate for anyone to get hurt."

The boys put a rope around my rear leg, drew it up toward my shoulder, and tied it around my neck.

Trussed this way, I had to hop around on three legs. But there was ample grass and fresh running water, and that was all I cared about for now.

When a man came and gave me bitter medicine, I stopped grazing and swallowed it. And when another came to file down my hooves, I did not object.

With every bite of grass and sip of water, I felt myself growing whole again. My ribs disappeared beneath a silken pelt of hair. One day, a dog limped up to the fence.

How does it feel to get along on only three legs? he asked.

I lifted my head and looked him over. He was missing one of his hind legs. *At least I'll be getting my fourth leg back,* I snorted.

The dog bared his teeth in a smile. *You got*

me there, girlie. I lost mine beneath the wheels of a runaway coal wagon. The name used to be Shep. Now it's Tripod.

Good to meet you, Tripod. My name's Cinders.

He sat down on his bad hip to scratch a flea. *Is that a fact? Folks are saying it's Man-Killer.*

I heaved a sigh. *That's what they call me. I've been hearing it for so long I'm beginning to believe it.*

Well, I guess it's up to you to prove them wrong, isn't it? Just like I did when I came here.

How so? I asked.

I used to herd sheep. But after the accident, the rancher fired me because I was useless. Finn stepped in and saved me from getting a bullet in the head. I was so grateful, I wanted to repay Finn by proving my usefulness. I got my chance the night the wolf came around.

Wolf! My head jerked up from the grass. For the first time since coming here, I felt nervous. A horse is vulnerable enough on four legs. On three, she's an easy target.

Don't worry. I ran him off. I saved the life of a blind donkey.

Did you say blind donkey? I asked.

A wingless duck and a crippled goat, too. Take a good look around you. Nearly every animal here has something wrong with them, including you.

I glanced over to where the herd of Percherons stood in the shade of the trees, tails swatting at flies. *What's wrong with* them? I asked.

Nothing, really, said Tripod. *But keep watching and you'll see an amazing sight. Because today is Sunday, and Mrs. Finn is about to call everyone to go to church services down the road.*

Soon a woman came out onto the porch and rang a big silver bell.

Clang-clang-clang.

Over in the paddock, heads whipped up. The horses reared and snorted and shook their manes. They took off, galloping full tilt right up to the far

end of the pasture. There, they halted and lined
up along the fence, hooves planted, ears perked,
as if they were waiting for something very important to happen.

Then, after a moment or two, they shook
themselves down from mane to tail and went
back to being tired old horses.

They'll do it again next Sunday, Tripod said. They do it every time they hear a bell ring. See, they think it's the fire bell. They used to work for the fire department. In their day, they were heroes. They're retired now. But when they hear that bell, for a moment, they're young horses again, raring to risk their lives for the great city of Chicago.

5

Fall 1870: Miss Lizzy

One day, I watched as a young girl went into the paddock with the Percherons.

The horses were at the far end of the pasture, grazing. One look at her and they came stamped-ing down the hillside and surrounded her. The girl disappeared from sight. All I saw was a tight circle of horses facing in, their tails switching happily.

That would be Miss Lizzy, said Tripod.

Who is she?

She's Finn's niece from Chicago, Tripod said. *Her father, Michael Ryan, is Finn's brother. He's driver of the steam engine* Little Giant *out of the Maxwell Street fire station. She's got her father's guts and her uncle's way with animals. Come to think of it, she's got a way that's all her own.*

What do you mean? I asked.

You'll see, said Tripod as he went off in search of shade.

A few moments later, I looked up from the grass and there she was. At close range, she looked small and defenseless, with her flyaway golden hair. But there was a light shining out of her big pale eyes that made her seem larger and stronger.

Most humans who came into my pen were nervous for fear that the Man-Killer within me would stir awake and, even hobbled, strike out. But this girl had no fear. She walked right up to me and stuck out her hand.

"I saved one for you, Cinders," she said.

I hopped over and sniffed at the thing in her palm. It smelled delicious.

"Go ahead and take it. You'll like it," she said. "It's a horse cookie. I baked it myself, from sweet bran, grated carrots, molasses, and applesauce."

With quivering lips, I took the cookie into my mouth. It was crunchy and yet so soft that it melted on my tongue. I licked my lips, then roamed her palm in search of crumbs.

She wiped off her hands. "Sorry, girl. Those hungry heroes over there cleaned me out."

I followed her with my eyes as she walked slowly around me.

"You look much better than when Uncle Finn first brought you here. Now that you're on the mend, Uncle Finn wants to put you into the paddock with the old fire horses. But I told him that was a bad idea. You'd be very unhappy there. Their lives are over and yours is just beginning."

I hopped on my three legs as I tried to keep her in my sights.

"But you've suffered so much, haven't you?" she said, arriving at my head again and moving in so close all I could see was those eyes of hers.

"They think you're a killer, but I don't believe

it for a second." She stroked my ears and the sides of my head. "I think that, whatever happened, it was all a big misunderstanding. I think you're a *sweetheart*."

I leaned into her, hankering after a hug. She threw her arms around me. It felt wonderful to be embraced again!

At length, she pulled away and pointed to my leg. "We need to get that thing off. A good horse like you shouldn't be hobbled."

I held still as she reached up and picked at the knot that pulled my leg toward my shoulder.

After a few moments, she gave up. "The boys tied it too tight. I'll go get help."

She ran into the house. When she didn't come back, I stopped waiting for her. But the warmth of her hug stayed with me.

Eventually, she did come, bringing a man who looked and sounded like Finn but smelled like smoke. It brought back memories of Bud's blasting powder and the brush fires the old man used to set all too close to my paddock.

"If it isn't the notorious Percheron, Cinders!" he said.

"Isn't she gorgeous?" she asked.

"She's a good-looking animal, all right," he said. "But some of the meanest horses I ever met were good-lookers. Give me an ugly plug with a good disposition any day."

"Oh, Daddy, she's got a *sweet* disposition!" she said. "She'll be perfect."

"Oh, she will, will she?" he said.

"You'll see," she said.

He shook his head. "I don't know, Lizzy, my girl."

"The first thing we have to do is free her leg. Please, Daddy?" she begged.

With a sigh, he set to work on the knot.

"Then we need to take her with us back to the fire station. We can't leave her here another day. This is no place for a healthy young horse. She's a workhorse, Daddy. She needs to work. She'll feel better if she's useful. Won't you, Cinders?"

Just then, I felt the rope give way and my leg came free. Trembling and twitching, I lowered it to the ground.

"That leg is bound to be a little sore for a while," Lizzy said. "You'll need to regain your balance. Even though it hurts, put your weight on it to get the blood moving again."

"Honey," said the man, "I think we need to go and let Cinders get used to having four legs again."

"No, Daddy. Cinders wants to show you what she can do, don't you, Cinders?"

The man gave me a wide-eyed look. "Oh, she does, does she?"

"Please, Daddy?"

Sighing, the man began to put his hands on me. He knew his way around a horse. I responded as promptly and smoothly as my stiff leg would allow. All my moves came back to me in a sweet rush.

I backed up. I came forward. I moved from side to side. I turned in a circle on my hind legs. I turned on my forehand. When I was finished, I did the trick the Little Ones taught me just before they went away. I bent over my front legs and bowed.

Miss Lizzy clapped her hands.

"Did you see that, Daddy! She knows! She knows everything a horse ought to know—and more!"

Michael stood back and put his fists on his hips and frowned. "Somebody, somewhere, sometime put some serious training on you," he said to me.

"Uncle Finn says she was trained to pull a plow and a wagon and a sled and everything. She'll make a *fine* fire horse. With a name like Cinders, how could she not?"

"But what about that business back in DeKalb?" he said.

"That was an *accident,* Daddy. It wasn't her fault. I know it."

He eyed her closely. "You do, do you?"

"She told me so with her eyes, and horses' eyes never lie, Daddy."

6

Fall 1870: Chicago

The city came at me from every angle, dirty and noisy and rude, sending me skittering from side to side behind the wagon I was tied to.

Lizzy, neck craned, watched me with worried eyes.

"Stop the wagon, Daddy. I need to calm Cinders down."

"It's almost dark, and I told your mother I'd have you home early. It's the first day of school tomorrow."

"But you promised I could go with Cinders to the fire station!" she said.

"I know I did, but traffic was heavier than I thought and I need to get you home."

"But she'll be scared without me."

"If she's going to be a fire horse, she'll have to get used to a lot worse, won't she?"

Lizzy's eyes said, *I'm so sorry, Cinders!*

And the look I returned said, *Me too!*

Michael turned onto a narrow street and pulled up before a small wooden house. A woman

waited at the door. Lizzy ran back and hugged me
hard.

"Be brave, Cinders!" she whispered. "I'll come
and visit as soon as Mother lets me."

Then she ran into the house.

As we made our way down the narrow road, I craned my neck, eyes on the house. Finally, I found Lizzy, standing at one of the windows. I whickered. She waved sadly.

When we arrived at the fire station, more men smelling of smoke came pouring out of the big wooden building.

"Say hello to Cinders, lads, our new fire horse," Michael told them.

I heard horses muttering from somewhere in the back. Two spotted dogs sniffed around my hooves.

"Dumpling's stall is all cleaned out," one of the men said.

My ears swiveled. There was that word *stall*.

I vowed never to enter another stall as long as I lived.

Michael tugged on my lead rope. I planted my hooves and refused to move. Michael tugged harder.

In their stalls, the horses were gossiping about me. I tried not to listen. I wasn't going to be staying, anyway. Without Lizzy, I had no business being in this place.

Another man said, "I thought we agreed we had enough horses for now."

Michael said, "If, God forbid, something happens to Butch, we've got backup. Now, Joe, get behind her and push."

"Is this horse even *broke*?" Joe asked.

Michael said, "Broke *and* trained. She just

needs to adjust. I see now I should have let Lizzy stay. She'd get this horse moving, meek as a lamb."

"Yeah, but Lizzy can't live here, and now this meek lamb is *our* problem."

"Keep pushing, Joe!" Michael said.

"Sakes alive, Michael Dolan! She's a ton of horseflesh. If she doesn't want to move, no amount of pushing will get her going. How much did we pay for her, may I ask?"

"She was free," said Michael.

"Well, there you go. You get what you pay for," said Joe.

"She's a valuable animal, she is. Trained Percherons cost a fortune. Fetch a bucket of feed now and go stand in her stall, like a good lad," said Michael.

Joe went to stand in the empty stall. He

banged the bucket with the scoop. I smelled the oats, sweet and tangy, but I would not be bribed.

Instead of moving toward the bucket, I backed away from it, dragging Michael with me. I backed out of the fire station doors and into the middle of the street. I wanted to keep going all the way back to Second Chance Farm, where I had sweet grass and my own stream.

Outside, I found nothing familiar. Where was the soft darkness of the country night throbbing with the sound of crickets? The street was crammed with carts and wagons and people shouting and yelling. I was spooked nearly senseless.

"Get that stupid horse out of our way!" a voice rang out.

Another man hollered, "Hey! Isn't that the horse that killed Old Man Muller last winter?"

"Man-Killer!" someone else shouted.

And soon they were all chanting, "Man-Killer! Man-Killer!"

To hear that name again brought me pain as if a whip were stinging my back. My front hooves came off the ground. I was warming up for a good rear.

Inside the fire station, the dogs were barking. Michael hollered, "Chief! Get out here!"

One of the spotted dogs came bounding out of the shadows.

"Make yourself useful, girl. Calm this horse down and drive her into her stall," he said.

The dog walked up to me. *Look, missy*, she said. *I don't know how you do things where you come from. But here we don't carry on this way. Any minute now, that bell is going to ring and we'll*

be rushing off to do serious work. This is no place to throw silly tantrums.

I settled down and licked my lips. I suddenly knew that this little dog, more than all the boys smelling of smoke, was in charge here. I waited for my orders.

That's more like it, she said. *Now let's get a move on.* Coming up behind me, she snapped her jaws. I took a step forward.

Don't stop now, she said to me.

With that little spotted dog on my tail, I trotted back into the fire station and, for better or for worse, into the stall.

All Ears and a Dozen Spots

The Maxwell Street fire station was a busy, noisy place. The same routine happened almost every day and even some nights. Sparky, which was the name of the dog who was in charge, would bark and dance around and then a loud bell would ring.

The doors of the stalls to either side of me would slide open and the horses would spring out. They trotted forward: the three white mares lining themselves up in front of one wagon, the black Percheron in front of the other. Harnesses

and collars dropped down from the ceiling, already attached to the wagons' traces. Boys came along and hooked up the harnesses and attached the reins.

While all this was happening, more boys came

clomping down the stairs from somewhere up above. They jumped into their boots and clapped on their helmets. Then, together, horses, men, and the two dogs—Sparky and her mother, who was called Blaze—all dashed off to who knew where.

While they were gone, peace and quiet settled over the fire station. I often dozed. But I woke up as soon as they came jogging back, tired and dirty and smelling strongly of smoke.

The first thing they would do was clean up. The men paid special attention to the horses. They hosed them down and soaped them up and even cleaned their teeth with a big wooden brush. The horses were then dried off and put away in their stalls with grain and hay.

But before very long, Sparky would bark and

dance and the whole chain of events would start up all over again. It bothered me that, as many times as they did this, no one ever invited me to join in.

One morning, I was standing with my head in the back of my stall, sulking about this very thing.

Behind me, Sparky asked, *Do you actually enjoy feeling sorry for yourself?*

I sighed and ignored her.

Why am I even here? I wondered aloud.

You're here to be a fire horse, said Sparky. *Don't worry. They'll get around to training you one of these days. They're giving you a chance to settle in. Say, is it true what they say? That you're a man-killer?*

Joints creaking, I turned around slowly.

I'm no man-killer! I said sadly.

Is that a fact? Well, suppose you tell me your side of the story, she said. *I'm all ears and a dozen spots.*

I drew myself up tall and began. I have to admit, it felt good to finally unburden myself. I explained what had happened the fateful night of the winter storm. I told her about the freezing trip home, the old man pitching forward over the dashboard, the sons bullying me and forcing me to step on him. I told her about all the things, bad and good, that had happened to me since then.

When I finished my tale, she said, *I'll tell you what I think. I think this fire station is as good a place as any for you to get a fresh start. If you give us a chance, we'll give you one.*

The next day, as if he knew I was ready, Michael came to my stall with lead rope and halter in hand.

"All right, then, Cinders," he said. "Are you ready to learn how to be a fire horse and do my Lizzy proud?"

I stood back and let him halter me up and take me out.

When he was finished grooming me, he took me for a walk around the block.

The sights and sounds didn't bother me nearly as much as they had when I first arrived. To begin with, it was daytime. Everything is less frightening in the sunlight. And, besides, I had spent the last few weeks in my stall getting used to these sounds.

Little children, sensing my ease, came up to

pet me. Dogs sniffed at my hooves. Cats rubbed up against my feathered fetlocks.

When Michael returned me to the stable after our walk, the horse in the stall next to mine asked, *Did you have a pleasant stroll?*

I turned to the beautiful white Thoroughbred mare who, up until this moment, had all but ignored me. *Oh, hello,* I said to her. *Yes, it's good to get out and stretch my legs again.*

I've got a feeling, said the identical Thoroughbred one stall down from the first, *you're going to be stretching those legs plenty in the next months. I'm Daisy, and the mare next to you is Maisy. The gal on my other side is Maybelle.*

Maybelle, an exact copy of Daisy and Maisy, nodded to me. *My pleasure, I'm sure.*

We pull the Little Giant, said Maisy.

Which is to say the steam engine, said Daisy.

The most important piece of equipment in the fire station, said Maybelle.

Making us the most important horses here, said Daisy.

The black Percheron on my other side snorted, *You stuck-up gals! What makes you think you're so special? The steam engine might pump the water, but you can't put a fire out without a hose. The name's Butch. I pull the hose cart.*

Pleased to meet you, Butch, I said.

Speaking for all of us, said Butch, I'm awfully glad you've come.

Maybelle said, *We overheard you telling your troubles to Sparky. We know now you're not a man-killer.*

And I'm sure you'll make a fine fire horse, said Maisy.

Welcome to the herd, said Butch.

The next day began with Sparky barking and the bell going off. For the first time, the door to my stall slid open. All the other stall doors stayed closed. No men came sliding down the pole to jump into their uniforms. That's when I knew that my training had begun.

Michael and Sully, the hose cart foreman, each took one side of my halter and walked me out of the stall to stand in front of the hose cart. The next moment, a collar and harness dropped down from the ceiling onto my back.

I had seen this go on with the other horses,

but I spooked when it first happened to me. I soon settled down and let the men fasten on the collar and harness. When they tried to put the blinkers on me, they discovered what Farmer Zeke had once learned: I do not need blinkers and I will not tolerate them. I shook my head until they slid down on my face. So there.

"It appears our gray lady doesn't favor blinkers," said Sully.

"So much the better," said Michael.

They harnessed me up many times over. And when I could undergo it without a single twitch, Michael gave me a lump of sugar and said, "Good girl, Cindy!"

I smacked the sugar into my lips. Cindy! That was a much sweeter name than Man-Killer.

A few days later, I went through the same drill, but the boys added some steps. Once my collar was fastened, the boys led me, hose cart in tow, out the fire station door into the street.

Soon I could go through all the steps: exit the stall and trot up in front of the hose cart; hold still while the harness and collar were fastened; exit the fire station pulling the cart; get my lump of sugar and my "Good girl, Cindy!"

When I could do this quickly and smoothly, Michael laid a rope along the floor. The next time Sparky barked and the bell went off, there were no boys to guide me.

At first, I hesitated. Then I looked down and saw the rope laid out on the floor. Like a trail, it led from my stall to the front of the hose cart and then out the door.

Sparky said, *You get the idea. Follow the rope.*

I did exactly that and got an extra lump of sugar.

After that, Sully hitched me up to the hose cart and began to take me on runs through the city. Sparky always went with me to guide me and clear the way.

Following one of these runs, I asked Sparky a question that had been nagging at me for some time.

So, now that I've told you my big secret, can you tell me yours?

What secret? she asked, scratching a flea.

I notice that every time you dance around and bark, the bell rings, I said.

She chuckled. *I don't make it ring. I just know when it's going to go off. I get a tingling feeling in my bones.*

I wondered if the tingling feeling came from her spots. I had spots, too. Would my own spots soon start to tingle in advance of the fire bell?

Do you think that maybe someday I'll get that tingling feeling, too?

You never know, said Sparky.

The endless practice—getting all gussied up in harness with no real fire to go to—was beginning to bore me. I was eager to prove my worth to Michael and the boys, to Sparky, and to the other horses.

One day, Lizzy came to visit. She stood against the wall of the fire station, holding a shiny metal disk.

That thing in her hand is a watch, Sparky explained. *It tells her how quickly you can get ready to go to a fire.*

I wanted to show Lizzy just how fast I could be. When Sparky started barking and the bell rang, Lizzy clicked the watch, and out the stall door I charged.

I trotted forward smartly and stood in front of the hose cart. The collar and harness came down on me, and Sully buckled them into place. Lizzy jumped up and down and cheered. As I pulled the wagon out the fire station door, she clicked the watch again. Sparky barked with joy.

"Daddy! Come and see!" She held up the watch. "That's forty-five seconds! A Maxwell Street record!"

Michael looked at the watch. "Well, I'll be . . . ," he said. "You were right about Cinders, Lizzy."

After they unhitched me and took off my harness, Lizzy groomed me. "I know you're impatient. You want to get out and go. But my father says you need at least another six months of practice. That seems like forever to you. But that's the way they do things on Maxwell Street."

When she put me back in my stall, she gave me three horse cookies fresh from the oven. I gobbled them down, one right after another, and licked my lips.

Before she left, she hugged me and whispered, "Be patient, Cinders. Your day will come."

As it turned out, I would not have long to wait.

8

1871: A Devilish Wind

The air in the fire station always smelled smoky. But by my second year there, it reeked of burning wood as well. There was almost always a fire breaking out somewhere in the city. The horses were scarcely cleaned up from the last fire when the bell went off calling them to the next one.

Then out of the stalls they would spring. Down the stairs the men would pound. And off they'd go, returning hours later with faces and arms blackened with soot. I asked Butch one day, *Are all Chicago summers this bad?*

This is the worst I've seen, Butch said.

It's the heat, said Daisy.

And the drought, said Maisy.

There's been almost no rain at all, said Maybelle.

The fall brought no relief. The heat and the dryness were bad enough. But on some days, a powerful wind, like the bellows in a smithy, blew from off the prairie. On the street outside the fire station, stray papers and dried leaves rattled past.

It's a devilish wind, said Butch. *Who knows what it will blow our way?*

What with our cold-weather coats coming in,

we horses sweated and itched beneath our winter-weight fur.

Then, one hot, windy day, Sparky started barking and doing her Fire Dance. Everyone was hoping that, just this once, she was wrong.

But Sparky was never wrong. The bell went off.

I've got a bad feeling about this, Butch grumbled, just before his stall door slid open. He and the others stepped out and went through their paces with hooves dragging.

If only someone would slide open *my* door, I'd leap at the chance to join them. I was fresh and ready. But as always, they went off and left me in my stall. What a waste of horsepower!

I waited for their return. But they didn't come back. I paced in a circle.

Fat Belle, the fire station ratter, leaped onto the ledge of Butch's empty stall.

You're as nervous as a big cat in a small cage, she said.

They've been gone for so long, they've missed my feeding.

I stopped pacing, and my ears swiveled forward as another alarm went off.

Uh-oh, said Belle. *Two alarms. That's not good.*

Moments later, more wagons from other stations went clattering through the streets on their way to the fire.

I resumed my pacing only to pull up short as a third alarm sounded.

Not good at all, said the cat. *At the rate this is going, half the crews in town will be called out.*

When a second feeding time had passed, I fell into a doze to the sound of my stomach rumbling and gurgling.

Late the next morning, Sparky came dragging in, looking like someone had dunked her in a vat of tar.

It was a bad one, she said as she hacked up a puddle of black goo.

The others, boys and horses, followed. Blaze came limping in last.

I burned my paw pads. I tell you, I don't know how much longer I can do this, she said. She sat down on the floor and started licking her wounded paws.

The boys unhitched the horses, hosed them down, and put them in their stalls with feed and hay.

"You missed a bad one, Cindy," Michael told me when he came into my stall to give me my oats.

Sparky and Blaze, having bathed in the run-off from the hoses, shook themselves dry and went upstairs to find some chow.

Most of the boys soon followed. I heard them fall into their bunks like sacks of rocks, too worn out to eat or wash up.

Buckets banging, we ate our oats, then started in on our hay. Soon the others were fast asleep, snoring softly. But I was still awake.

I noticed that one horse remained outside. It was Butch, standing in the crossties. Sully was fussing over him.

I called out to Butch, *Are you okay?*

I hurt! Butch called back.

When Michael returned to top off my water, I trotted out of the stall, over to Sully, and parked my nose on his shoulder.

He turned to me. "Oh, hey there, Cindy."

I snorted. I wasn't there to be friendly. I wanted him to know that I had my eye on him. Butch had some serious burns on his back. I wanted to make sure Sully did the job properly.

Sparky had joined us. *Poor old Butch*, she said.

Butch's hide twitched at Sully's touch.

I nickered. *Is this man hurting you? Say the word and I'll run him off.*

He's not hurting me, Butch said. *It's the burns that hurt. You should have seen it. There was a whoosh,* followed by this tremendous boom! *Everybody spooked!*

Sparky said, *The roof of a warehouse collapsed in an explosion of embers. Some of them landed on Butch. He bucked and rolled, but they burned into his hide.*

"I don't know, Mike," said Sully. "These burns are bad. I think we need to put Butch on the Sick List."

"Sure, it's the right thing to do," said Michael, "even though that leaves us down one horse."

"I guess we'll just have to manage with what we've got," said Sully, leading Butch back to his stall.

"All I can say," said Michael, "is there had better not be any more fires in this town until he's all healed up."

Before Sully went upstairs, he walked me back to my stall and fiddled with my door. I knew what he was doing. He was rigging it to spring open the next time the bell rang.

It made my heart glad.

When Sparky barked and did her Fire Dance later that same day, I snapped to attention. The bell rang. Upstairs, I heard the boys groaning. Moments later, they came staggering down the stairs. Meanwhile, the stall doors slid open and the four of us trotted out. I was the first horse to be hitched up, taking Butch's place in front of the hose cart.

"I'm glad *somebody* around here's got some spunk," said Sully as he clipped on my reins. "Come on, Cindy girl, let's go put out a fire."

"Where's Michael?" someone shouted.

"He went out to dinner with some friends," Joe shouted back.

"He hates missing a fire," said Jack.

"Doubtless he'll hear the bell wherever he is and come running like always," said Joe.

How can I describe the thrill I felt as, wind whipping my mane, I cantered through the streets of Chicago pulling the hose cart with Sparky dashing at my side?

A man swept off his hat and called out to Sully, "I see you've got yourself a fine new dappled horse!"

Sully called back, "That I do! This is her first fire."

"Good luck to the both of you!"

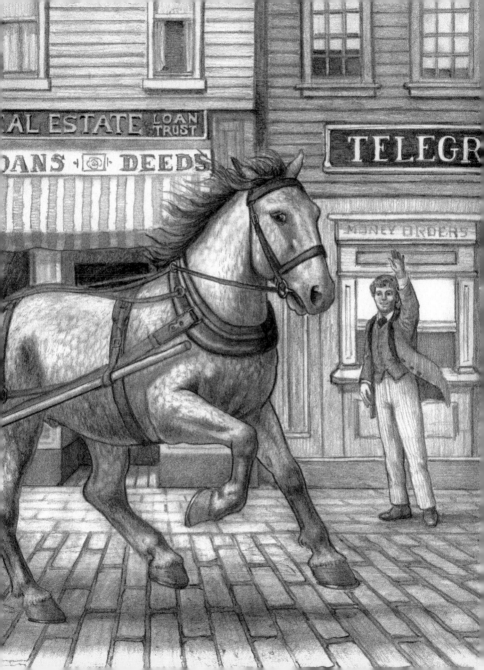

Behind us was the *Little Giant*, with Joe at the reins Michael usually held.

The courthouse tower bell tolled. Sully shook his head and said to Jack, "Wrong, wrong, wrong. The bell is *wrong*. It's sending out the *wrong* signal. It's sending crews to the *wrong* address," Sully muttered darkly. "We're off to a very poor start tonight."

I didn't like the way this sounded. I felt my first twinge of unease.

Don't let it bother you, Sparky said. *Men make mistakes.*

As soon as we arrived on the scene, the heat of excitement in my blood turned to icy-cold fear. A barn and some sheds were ablaze. I had seen fires on the farm, but never anything this big. It was hot and bright and shockingly loud. For this, there had been no training.

Sparky said, *Now you know that being a fire horse means more than looking lively at the sound of the bell. It also means staying calm in the face of fire. I learned to do it. And you'll learn, too.*

This was easier said than done. Fire was a living, breathing thing—an evil force that meant me harm. I jigged in place.

"Easy now, Cinders," Sully said. He hopped out and unhitched me, leading me away from the heat.

"Keep an eye on the greenhorn, Sparky," he said as he began to unravel the hose from the wagon.

I tossed my head and shifted my weight onto

my hind legs, braced to run. Now was the time. But something stopped me. Somehow I knew that if I ran away now, I'd be something almost as hateful as Man-Killer. I'd be a failure!

Men dashed to and fro, bumping heads and tripping over each other's hoses. They flailed about like a herd of horses without a leader.

What's happening? I asked Sparky, panic seizing me in spurts that I constantly had to fight down.

They're looking for fireplugs. They get water from the city's mains through the fireplugs. The steam engine pumps it out and shoots it through the hoses. Sometimes, when a burn is big and there are lots of men and equipment, there aren't enough plugs to go around.

Is this a big burn? I asked.

It looks like it, said Sparky. *Who knows? It might even be the Big Burn. The one Michael said was going to come sooner or later, because Chicago is built mostly out of wood, and fire loves wood.*

Fire loves horses, too! my inner voice screamed. *But I must not let it have me.*

I was relieved to see Michael come running, still buttoning up his jacket and shouting. His fearlessness lent me some calm. He set to work, running a short hose from the plug to the *Little Giant* and then attaching one end of Sully's hose to the steam engine. Soon the hose filled with water. It wriggled along the ground like a big fat snake.

Where did Sully go? I asked Sparky.

He's down the alley at the other end of that hose. He's getting closer to the fire, Sparky said.

Is there always this much confusion? I asked.

No, she said. *Tonight's different. Everything's going wrong. The lads are tired, the equipment is dirty, and the alarms are wrong. The wind is the worst I've ever seen. You watch yourself, Cinders. If the wind blows an ember on you, shake it off or drop down and roll. You don't want to wind up like poor Butch.*

The very idea made me shiver all over.

That's the idea, big girl, said Sparky. *Listen, I'm spread thin tonight, what with Mum being on the Sick List. I need to check on the Thoroughbreds. Will you be all right by yourself, Cinders?*

Please don't go! I cried, but Sparky was already on her way over to check on the white mares.

My head craned this way and that as the wind whipped my mane. The fire seemed to be spreading fast. I hoped that Sparky would return soon, before it got me.

Suddenly, a giant of a man in a high peaked helmet came charging down the street.

"Let's get ourselves organized, boys!" he shouted.

I sensed immediately that this was the leader of all the firemen. The giant started speaking through a shiny horn that made his voice louder than the roar of the fire. He clapped one hand on his helmet to keep the wind from snatching it off his head.

"Move that hose!" the giant shouted.

"Soak that sidewalk!" he ordered.

"Keep moving and don't stop," he cried.

"Get as close as you can, lads!" he hollered.

"Give it all you've got!" he urged.

To his every command, the firemen said, "Yes, sir, Chief Fire Marshal Williams."

The boys went scurrying in all directions. Fires had broken out up and down the road. They flared and danced and crackled and roared something fierce, like nothing I had ever seen or heard before. I planted my hooves and held my ground. It took everything I had to keep from jumping out of my skin.

I looked over at the other horses. They tossed their manes and jogged in place. It was small comfort that they seemed as spooked as I was.

Suddenly, after the chief fire marshal barked an order at him, one of the firemen spun away from the fire and turned the spray on the row of buildings behind us. Sparky and the mares got soaked, too. They shook themselves off but seemed glad of it. Maybe the water kept them from bursting into flames. I didn't much like water, but I wished someone would come along and spray me. My breath deepened to a breathy wheeze. *Help me, someone!*

Above the din, I heard Daisy call out to Sparky, *This is getting bad!*

Maisy said, *The fire is coming closer to us!*

What if the men are too busy to take care of us? said Maybelle.

If we have to, we'll cut and run, said Daisy.

I cried out, *Don't leave without me!*

Sparky called over to me, *Nobody's going anywhere! Everybody, stay calm! I'm going to take a look around and see what's going on. Try to keep your heads while I'm gone.*

I couldn't believe she was leaving us. I called out to her, but the little dog disappeared into a wall of smoke and flames.

Come back soon! the other mares cried out.

The streets were suddenly crammed with people and wagons. A gasp went up, and the crowd scattered. A horse with snapped reins came stampeding through, followed by two terrified goats, a donkey with a smoking tail, and a bunch of flapping ducks.

Run for your lives! the horse shrieked, its eyes wild.

I looked to the others. *Should we go with them?* I called out to them.

No. Stay calm and wait for Sparky! Daisy called back.

Sparky will take care of us when she returns, Maisy said.

Oh, please come soon, I muttered as I danced from foot to foot. Oh, how I itched to run! But where would I run? The fire was everywhere.

My heart leaped with gladness when, at last, I spied Sparky making her way back to us.

Then one of the mares cried, *Look out behind you, Sparky!*

A strange man swooped down and tied a rope to Sparky's collar. He dragged her away with him.

We looked on helplessly as Sparky disappeared into the crowd. Where was that man taking her?

Without our fire dog, what would become of us?

The Little Lion

I was just running over to join the mares when two strange firemen came and led them off. Where were they going? First Sparky and now the herd. I was all alone!

I waited for someone to come for me, but no one paid me any mind.

The wind gusted and drove a red blizzard of embers into my face. I shook my mane hard. *This is it, Cinders,* I told myself. *It's time to cut and run before you catch fire and burn down to* real *cinders.*

Then a deep, raspy voice said, *Don't do it.*

For a moment, I froze. Then I looked down.

At first I thought it was some lady's mangy old fur coat that had been abandoned to the fire. Then, in the middle of the fur, I saw a pair of beady black eyes staring up at me.

Who are you? I asked.

I'm a dog, said the mangy ball of fur.

Really? Just knowing there was a dog somewhere in the middle of all that fur—no matter how odd he might sound or look—had a calming effect on me. I breathed out and licked my lips.

My name is Khan, also known as the Little Lion.
You're with the Maxwell Street outfit, aren't you?

I nodded.

I used to work for the butcher across the street.
Where are Blaze and Sparky? Khan asked.

Blaze is on the Sick List. A bad man just stole
Sparky. Is your tongue always this black, or did the
fire burn it?

I'm a chow chow, said Khan. *Some of us have*
dark tongues.

Are you a fire dog? I asked hopefully.

I'm a volunteer fire dog, he said.

What does that mean? I asked.

I love going to fires. I live on the street and go
where the fires are and help out where I can, said
the chow chow.

Please help me! I begged. *I'm terrified!*

Of course you are, said the Little Lion. *The first thing we need to do is move you out of harm's way. Don't look now. . . .*

I swung my head around and saw that the front wall of the building behind me was in flames and about to collapse on top of us.

Follow me! said Khan.

I ran after him down the block and around the corner. There, I saw the three Thoroughbreds pulling the *Little Giant* away.

I called out to them, *Where are you going?*

We're needed elsewhere! they called back. *Be of stout heart!*

The next moment, Sully came trudging up the alley doing my job, dragging the hose cart behind him.

"There you are, Cinders!" he said. "I was afraid I'd lost you."

While he was hitching me up, he noticed the strange dog.

"Is that you, Khan?"

Khan barked and wagged his tail.

"Well, what do you know? The Little Lion himself! I should have known you were the mystery chow chow dog that keeps showing up at fires. You always were a frustrated fire dog. Speaking of which . . ." He looked around. "Where's Sparky?"

Someone stole her! Khan and I both said together.

Sully shrugged. "I guess Sparky can take care of herself. But Cinders here I'm not so sure about. Khan, I'm on orders to head over to St. Paul's. If you come with us, maybe you can keep this mare from losing her head."

Khan grinned and panted.

"Come on, gang, let's get a move on!" said Sully.

Sully hopped up into the seat and grabbed the reins. "Walk on!"

Khan led us, zigzagging through streets roiling with people and animals. I'd hear the crackle and snap of burning wood, followed by a loud *whoosh-ing* sound. I'd plant my hooves and see that a new fire had started somewhere just ahead. Where was the fire coming from? No matter how far away we got from that first burning barn, the fire somehow managed to leap ahead of us.

I looked up. The sky was filled with burning spears. Whatever they landed on burst into flame. It was as if, suddenly, the fire was everywhere at once.

"Hang in there, Cinders, old gal!" Sully called out to me. "The church is right down the street."

The next moment, a building collapsed in

flames into the road directly before me. I pawed the ground and tossed my mane. Even with the wagon attached to me, I was ready to spin around and make a run for it.

"Whoa, girl!" said Sully, tugging firmly on the reins.

Easy does it, horsey, Khan rasped in my ear.

Slowly and carefully, Sully and Khan talked me around the flaming mountain. If it weren't for the two of them, I would have cut loose and run. We rounded the corner and I pulled up short and let out a shrill whinny. The spire of St. Paul's crumpled, and the burning shingles of the church roof caved in.

The chief fire marshal came running from the ruins. "You're too late here, but the match factory has just caught fire! The stable is next! The *Long*

John's over there, but her hoses have burned. We need to keep the fire from spreading to the lumberyard."

We rounded another corner, where the steam engine *Long John* was parked near a burning building that stood next to a stable. My nostrils quivered at the stench of burning horsehair. Sully went to talk to the driver, while Khan scampered into the stable.

Moments later, he came dashing out leading a string of horses, white-eyed and shiny with sweat. They kicked up their heels and ran off toward the river. Oh, how badly I wanted to join them!

Don't even think about it, said Khan, returning to my side. *Some of us have a job to do.*

The chief watched the runaway horses.

"God bless whoever let those poor devils free," he said.

The Little Lion just stood there, tongue lolling and fur steaming.

Sully came back to the cart and leaned on the hose reel. "The fire is winning, sir," he said to the commissioner.

"It's jumped the river, all right, and it's headed for the business district. Do the best you can here," said the chief.

Together, they grabbed the hose and started unwinding it from the reel.

I've got an idea! Khan said to me. *The hose cart horses on the South Side do this trick. Follow me, Cinders. Run!*

I was all too willing to run. I ran with Khan down the street. At first, Sully shouted at us to come back. Then he saw that the farther away we ran, the more of his hose came unwound from the reel. All he and the chief had to do was hold the pipe. We did the rest of the work for them.

Sully cupped his mouth and shouted, "A mighty fancy trick for a greenhorn!"

Give a dog a little credit, won't you? Khan grumbled. But I could tell he was pleased that the trick had worked.

But it didn't matter. All the hoses in the world couldn't put out the flames in the match factory. As much water as Sully and the other boys poured on it, the fire spread to the stable and, from there, to the lumberyards beyond.

All those stacks of green wood gave off an oily, thick smoke that stung my eyes and nostrils. Sully's eyes swelled nearly shut. His coat and whiskers were smoking. My legs were covered with burns. And Khan's fur was singed down to the skin in patches.

Sully fought on. The wind blew him, heavy hose and all, out into the middle of the road, where the flames licked at his sleeves. Finally, he dropped the hosepipe and gave up.

The fire had now turned on the *Long John*. The boys had to pull the steam engine back before the flames swallowed her whole. But her hose was still attached to the fireplug, and the fire had spread to it. The firemen couldn't get close enough to uncouple the hose.

Long John was trapped!

Her driver jumped into the driver's seat and flicked the whip. The team lunged forward and snapped the hose from the plug.

The hose flew up in the air, flipping and flopping like a snake dancing on its tail. The pipe whipped around and knocked Sully off his feet.

The foreman leaped down and ran to him. He slapped Sully's face. Sully sat up and shook his head. Soon he staggered to his feet, looking around for the next fire to fight.

It distressed me to no end to watch the men fight the fire on so many fronts and lose almost every time. For every fire they put out, ten new ones flared up to take its place. Up and down the river, everything, everywhere, was in flames. Khan and Sully and I kept the hose cart moving from one job to the next.

Explosions rocked the city. With each one, Sully would stop what he was doing and cock an ear.

"There goes the arsenal!" he said once with a sad shake of his head.

"That sounds like the gasworks!" he said another time.

Later, I heard a different sort of noise altogether. It was loud and hollow and deep and terrifying.

Sully said, "The courthouse just collapsed! I'd know the sound of that big bell anywhere!"

Buildings fell, trees burst into flame, and roofs blew off. The sky itself was lashed by tongues of fire. But when the most horrendous things happen enough times, even a horse eventually gives up and accepts them without flinching. That's what happened to me during that long night and

the following day. For the rest of my life, nothing ever spooked me again.

In the early hours of the morning, the boys were dumb with exhaustion and half blinded with smoke. Several times, Khan called on me to do the Hose Trick. We unspooled the hose and the boys hooked it up until, finally, the hose gave out and burst at the seams. But it didn't seem to matter because, not long after that, the central pumping station burned down.

With that, the fireplugs all around the city dried up.

Now there was no water left to fight with.

Chicago was at the mercy of the fire.

10

Burn Out

Early in the evening on the second day of the fire, Sully and Khan and I came limping into the fire station with nothing on the hose cart but an empty reel.

The Thoroughbreds were already there, along with the rest of the boys. Without water to pump, there was nothing to do now but come back and rest while the fire burned itself out.

I had to hand it to the boys. Tired and hurting though they were, they took care of us first.

Except for the steady but distant roar of the wind and the fire, all was quiet. Nobody seemed to have much to say.

In the middle of brushing down Daisy, Michael stopped suddenly and looked around. "Hey! Anyone seen Sparky?"

"I just saw her upstairs a few minutes ago," said Sully.

"That wasn't Sparky," said Joe. "That was Blaze. Blaze never went out. Sparky hasn't come back."

The men fell quiet again.

After a while, Sully, who was wrapping my

legs in bandages, said, "Now that you mention it, I haven't seen her since we headed out for St. Paul's."

"Oh, she went missing well before that, she did," said Michael. He paused and then wiped the soot from his brow. "I guess maybe this time our girl didn't make it."

Boys and horses drooped.

"She was a fine fire dog, she was," said Michael.

"There was no one like her," said Joe.

"I'll always remember that Fire Dance of hers," said Michael. "Uncanny."

"It's a good thing I had the Little Lion with me," said Sully. "For a volunteer fire dog, he did pretty well. He even taught Cinders to do a trick with the hose cart."

All eyes turned to Khan. The chow chow was lying in the doorway with his hind end in the street, as if unsure whether to come or go.

"Come over here, chow dog," Sully said.

He poured some water from a thermos into a bowl. "Drink up."

Khan limped over and stuck his nose into the bowl. For a while, everyone watched him lap up the water.

"You remember how he used to chase after us whenever we turned out for a fire?" Michael asked. "He was a right pest, he was."

"I think he just wanted to go to a fire," said Sully.

"Well, I guess he finally got his wish," said Jack.

"Maybe we should adopt him . . . now that

Sparky's gone," said Sully. "The horses don't seem to mind him now, do they?"

"After what these ladies have been through in the last twenty-four hours," said Michael, "we could bring a real live fire-breathing dragon in here and they wouldn't bat an eye."

When they put us away, Khan came into my stall with me. I was so used to having him by my side, I would not have had it any other way. He curled up next to me on a bed of straw.

What's a strange-looking dog like you doing in a city like this? I asked him.

Oh, so you need a bedtime story now, do you?

I am a little too keyed up to sleep, I confessed.

Me, I could sleep for a month, he said with a black-tongued yawn. *But here's your story: We chow dogs are one of the oldest breeds on earth.*

We hail from the far-off land of China. My mother sailed to America on a ship from China. Her master came here to build the great railroad. One night, he lost my mother in a game of cards to a butcher from Chicago. The butcher brought her here, and not long after that, she whelped me. Growing up across from a fire station, I dreamed of being a fire dog. Last night, my dream came true.

Too bad it was such a nightmare for Chicago, I said. I dropped my head into my hay and started to munch. After a while, I heard the Little Lion snoring. Soon I was asleep, too.

Sometime in the night, I woke up to a gust of cool air blowing through the fire station. Moments later, big, wet drops of rain began hitting the street outside.

Over the sound of falling rain, I thought I

heard people cheering. Perhaps, I hoped, the rain had come to save us.

As I drifted off again, one last thought went through my head: Was this same rain falling on Sparky? And was she still alive to enjoy it?

The next morning, a wagon came rolling past the fire station and came to a halt. We were all out of our stalls, being bathed in the water that had filled up the rain barrel during the night.

A sooty young woman with singed hair and a ragged dress hopped down from the wagon. She ran and jumped into Michael's arms.

"Is it really you? You're alive!" he cried. "Your ma sent word that you'd gone missing! We've been out of our minds with worry, we have."

It was my dear old friend Lizzy!

"I fell out of the wagon and got lost, but then Sparky and I found each other. We've been through so much together," she said.

Then Michael looked at the wagon and said, "Chief?"

A black dog jumped down and ran to him.

"Is that my Sparky dog beneath all that soot?"

Sparky barked and danced.

For a moment, we all stiffened, afraid that the fire bell was about to go off. But this time, Sparky was just dancing for joy.

"And here we were fretting that the fire had claimed your spotted self," said Michael.

"It wasn't the fire," said Lizzy. "It was a looter. He dognapped Sparky. I found her way over on the north side, where I had fled from the fire. We helped each other."

Michael knelt down and rubbed Sparky until the soot began to come off and her spots showed through. "And to think that all this time you were looking after my Lizzy."

"Sparky's the best dog in the world," Lizzy said.

"Well, of course she is," said Michael. "She's a hero. With a hero's raging thirst, too, I bet."

He set down a bowl of rainwater and she lapped it up. When she was finished, she came over to greet the rest of us.

You missed all the excitement, said Maisy.

We'd given you up for lost, said Daisy.

We were fixing to mourn you, said Maybelle.

I kept my head down in a big mound of hay. I was still peeved at her for going off and leaving me to the mercy of the fire.

How did Cinders fare? Sparky asked.

Not bad, said Daisy.

Very well, in fact, said Maisy.

For a greenhorn, said Maybelle.

I raised my head from the hay. Sparky came over and touched her nose to mine.

I'm proud of you, Cindy, she said.

I flushed out my nostrils, then nuzzled her back. Who was I to hold a grudge for leaving me in the lurch? I was glad she was alive.

They say the Great Fire is giving Chicago a fresh start, she said. *And I guess the same is true for you.*

And what about me?

That's when Khan chose to come strutting out of my stall on his stiff little legs.

Sparky's back went up.

Michael put a hand on her head. "Easy, Chief. That scruffy fuzz ball showed up to do your job when you went missing. He turned out to be a good little volunteer fire dog, he did."

And just like that, Sparky's fur smoothed out and her tongue lolled. She went over and sniffed

Khan. *You smell worse than a burning dump pile,* she said.

You don't exactly smell like a rose yourself, said Khan, sniffing her back.

I will say no more, except to add that some time later—thanks to that scruffy fuzz ball—Sparky whelped a litter of nine of the strangest-looking pups you've ever laid eyes on.

Firemen from every house in Chicago lined up for a chance to adopt those pups, who all grew up to be first-rate fire dogs, just like their folks.

As for me, I remained at the fire station for many years. The boys made me a pet of sorts. I was the only horse allowed to wander loose. I put my nose into everyone's business. But I was happiest out on the sidewalk, dozing in the midday sun.

One day I was dozing when a woman's voice woke me. "This is Cinders," she said, "the mare your aunt Trudy and I had to leave behind when we weren't much older than you are. She turned out to be a famous fire horse. A real hero."

I opened my eyes to see a fine lady standing before me, holding the hand of a little girl. I offered my head for them to stroke and kiss.

"I told you she would remember me!" said the lady to the little girl. "We brought something for you, Cinders." Then she draped me in a garland made of sweet prairie flowers, and I knew who this was: Abby, the Little One who, along with her sister, had brushed out my coat and kissed my nose so many years ago. And for a brief, sweet time before they went away, I became her doll baby once more.

Not long after that, I bade farewell to the boys of the Maxwell Street fire station. I went to live with Daisy and Maisy and Maybelle and Butch and so many others in the big paddock at Second Chance Farm.

If you ever come looking for me, that's where you'll find me, eating grass and swatting the flies with my tail.

Except for on Sundays, when Lizzy—all grown up now, with Little Ones of her own—rings the bell. That's when our heads whip up. We rear and snort and shake our manes and take off together, galloping full tilt right up to the far end of the pasture.

There, we halt and line up along the fence, hooves planted, ears perked. For a few thrilling moments, we're young horses again, ready and raring to risk our lives to serve the great city of Chicago.

APPENDIX

The Big Burn

In 1871, Chicago was the fourth-largest city in America. Located on the western shores of Lake Michigan, it boasted a population of 334,000. The wealthier people lived in mansions in the city's southeast district. Poorer folks lived scattered about in shacks and tenements in the west, north, and south. The business district, located in the center of the city, included office buildings, department stores, theaters, opera houses, and grand hotels. Along the two branches of the Chicago River, which ran through the city, there were wharves, lumberyards, workshops, warehouses, coal yards, and bridges. Wood, sourced from the great forests to the north, was the primary building material. Even buildings made of stone were covered with wooden decorations. Wooden sidewalks raised pedestrians above the mud. Of the 538 miles of streets, only 88 miles were paved, and 57 of them were paved with wooden blocks. All in all, Chicago was a highly flammable city.

In the late 1800s, most towns and cities in America still had volunteer fire departments. But Chicago had 25 fire departments manned with 185 paid, trained professional firefighters. These men had their work cut out for them. In 1868 alone, 515 fires were recorded in the city—an average of two alarms every day.

There was an elaborate firefighting system. A central watchman, located in the tower of the courthouse, kept an eye out for fires. In addition, each fire station had a watchman. When the courthouse watchman spotted a fire, he rang the bell and telegraphed the fire stations closest to the blaze. If someone on the street spotted flames, they went to the nearest firebox to alert the courthouse, which notified the proper fire station. The giant courthouse bell tolled a code that broadcasted the fire's location. There were also special insurance patrols, men who patrolled the streets on foot, ready to put out small fires with extinguishers or turn on alarms for bigger blazes. So you might well ask, if Chicago was so well prepared, how did a small fire in a dairy barn result in a citywide disaster like the Great Fire?

The afternoon of Sunday, October 8, 1871, was unseasonably warm and dry. The summer-long drought had lasted into the fall. The trees drooped with dry leaves, and a steady wind from the southwest gusted and swirled. Just the day before, a sixteen-hour blaze had exhausted the city's firefighters and taxed their equipment, including most of the seventeen steam engines— all the city had.

We will never know for sure what started the fire, but we do know where it started: in Mrs. O'Leary's dairy barn, on the corner of DeKoven and Jefferson Streets. Legend has it that one of her cows kicked over a kerosene lantern. There was even a famous song written about it:

One dark night, when people were in bed,
Mrs. O'Leary lit a lantern in her shed,
The cow kicked it over, winked its eye,
    and said,
There'll be a hot time in the old town tonight.

Later, an official investigation revealed that the cow was probably not to blame, nor was Mrs. O'Leary, who had gone to bed early that night. Perhaps the story of the guilty cow survives in popular myth and imagination because it was such a simple explanation. But the real cause of the fire remains murky. One theory has it that guests of the O'Learys' tenants—who were having a party that night—went to the barn to get milk and accidentally kicked over the lantern. Another theory maintains that boys smoking and playing poker in the hayloft started it. Still another attributes the fire to a falling meteor! We do know that a friend of the O'Learys', Daniel "Peg Leg" Sullivan, testified that he called on the family at nine o'clock and discovered that they had all gone to bed. Sullivan had sat down to rest his stump when he spotted smoke. "Pat! Kate!" he shouted. "Your barn is on fire."

There was a firebox on the nearby corner, at Goll's Drugstore. Mr. Goll later said he sent in two alarms. But watchers at the courthouse claimed never to have received them. Was the firebox not working properly, or was Mr. Goll lying? We'll never know. But we do know that the courthouse watchers incorrectly pegged the location of the fire and repeatedly sounded the wrong alarms. Only two fire companies whose lookouts had spotted flames—Engine Company 6 (*Little Giant*), located on Maxwell Street, and Engine Company 5 (*U.P. Harris*), located on West Jackson Street—arrived right away. All the others went on a wild-goose chase, giving the fire a head start.

Within the first hour, the wind drove the fire into neighboring yards. Barns, houses, chicken coops, trees, sidewalks, and fences went up in flames. Neighbors helped residents pull furniture, clothes, and family members to safety while the flames leaped from roof to roof.

Chief Fire Marshal Robert A. Williams, the citywide head of the fire department, arrived to supervise. He ordered the men to surround the fire. But the fire jumped over their heads and fanned out. The wind whipped up the flames, causing a phenomenon known as a fire devil. As heated air rose and met cooler air, it began to spin like a tornado. The fire "devils" whirled, carrying sparks, burning firebrands, and debris, spreading the conflagration far and wide.

The fire advanced, unchecked. Embers fell, according to eyewitnesses, like "a blizzard of red snow." Some of them landed on St. Paul's Church, four blocks away from the O'Learys' barn. The steeple caught fire, and from there, the embers blew across the river into the business district and wealthy residential district. As the fire made its way through the city, it burned down shantytowns as well as mansions. It destroyed factories and businesses, hotels and department stores, theaters and

bridges and office buildings. When the city water-works burned down at three o'clock on Monday morning, the fire pumps stopped being able to draw water.

As Monday morning dawned, the mayor sent out an SOS: "Chicago in flames." Help soon came pouring in from Milwaukee, Cincinnati, Dayton,

Louisville, Detroit, Pittsburgh, and other cities. Despite all the efforts, the fire continued to run rampant. The streets were mobbed with looters, people fleeing the fire, and spectators watching in horrified fascination.

Thirty thousand homeless people flocked to Lincoln Park, on the shores of Lake Michigan. The fire burned all of Monday and well into the evening. It might well have gone on burning, too, were it not for the rain that started falling that night. The showers slowed down the spread long enough for firefighters to get the upper hand.

By the time the fire was out, it had destroyed an area four miles long and a mile wide, burning 18,000 buildings and 73 miles of street. It killed 300 people and left another 100,000 homeless. Newspaper writers called it the Great Fire.

Want to know more about the Great Chicago Fire? Go to chicagohs.org.

Did Mrs. O'Leary's cow start the fire? Visit this site to read an in-depth investigation: greatchicagofire.org.

An Ancient Breed

The Percheron gets its name from the district in northern France known as Le Perche, where the breed is said to date back to the last Ice Age. Over the centuries, people used the Percheron to do farmwork. In 732, when the Moors invaded during the Battle of Tours, Arabian blood was mixed with Percheron. Perhaps it is the Arabian strain that accounts for the Percheron's distinctive combination of strength and grace.

The Percheron is black or gray and ranges in height from fifteen to nineteen hands and weighs between 1,400 and 2,600 pounds. A willing worker with a good disposition, it also has enormous stamina, enabling it to travel up to thirty-five miles a day at a trot! Owing to its size, strength, and intelligence, the Percheron was the breed favored by firemen to haul

heavy equipment in the days before motorized vehicles.

For more information about Percherons, visit percheronhorse.org.

Heroes on the Hoof

In 1832, New York's Mutual Hook & Ladder Company No. 1 purchased a horse. It was probably the first official fire horse. Up until this time, firemen carried their own tools or hauled them in a wagon. But as cities grew larger, firefighting equipment got heavier, so horses became a necessity.

Why horses? Horses are sensitive creatures that spook easily, and fires are terrifying. But firemen maintained that a properly trained horse was as good as gold. In fact, it cost ten times the salary of a single fireman to buy and train a fire horse over a two-year period. And not just any horse would do. The horse had to be smart and strong and sure-footed. The Percheron was the breed most commonly chosen, but draft horses, saddlebreds, and Thoroughbreds were also used.

The city of Detroit even had a "college" devoted exclusively to training horses. But in most cases, firemen trained horses at their own stations. Learning to stay calm and cool at the site of a fire, however, was something that only came to a horse with on-the-job experience. And that experience was often scary and dangerous. Running across cobblestones or ice and snow, horses sometimes slipped and fell on the way to a fire. Or, like the firemen they worked with, they got burned—sometimes fatally. Because the job was so stressful and dangerous, the career of a fire horse was usually between four and eight years.

With the invention of motorized engines in the early 1900s, firefighters no longer needed horses to pull their equipment. After sixty years of brave and valiant service, fire horses became a thing of the past.

Check out this site dedicated to keeping the memory of fire horses alive: firehorses.info.

Cinders and the horses of the Maxwell Street fire station are fictional characters. To read about some actual fire horses in history, go to: equitrekking.com/articles/entry/famous_horses _in_history_-_the_fire_horse.

From Coach Dogs to Fire Dogs

Built for speed and endurance, Dalmatians have served as sporting dogs, war dogs, ratters, shepherds, and coach dogs. Here in America, Dalmatians are best known as fire dogs. Their job was to run alongside the fire horses, helping them stay on course and not spook, either on the way to the fire or once they were on-site. Fires are noisy, scary places, and horses are high-strung. There was something about the Dalmatians that kept the horses calm and steady.

In the years since motorized trucks have replaced horses, firefighters still keep Dalmatians as firehouse mascots, in memory of how it was in the old days.

For more information on this wonderful breed, visit akc.org/dog-breeds/dalmatian.

ABOUT THE AUTHOR

Kate Klimo wakes up every morning and mucks out the paddock and stalls of her two horses, Harry (a paint gelding) and Fancy (a quarter-horse mare). Kate and her husband (who is also named Harry) like to ride as often as they can on the trails of Mohonk Preserve, behind their house in New Paltz, New York, where the footing is great and the views are spectacular. They go on horseback-riding vacations once or twice a year and have ridden all over the world, from South Africa to Costa Rica, from Patagonia to Iceland. There is no day that is so bad, Kate claims, that it can't be vastly improved by getting on the back of a good horse. When she isn't riding, she is writing. She is the author of the Dog Diaries books and the Dragon Keepers series.

ABOUT THE ILLUSTRATOR

Ruth Sanderson grew up with a love for horses. She has illustrated and retold many fairy tales and likes to feature horses in them whenever possible. Her book about a magical horse, *The Golden Mare, the Firebird, and the Magic Ring,* won the Texas Bluebonnet Award.

Ruth and her daughter have two horses, an Appaloosa named Thor and a quarter horse named Gabriel. She lives with her family in Massachusetts.

To find out more about her adventures with horses and the research she does to create Horse Diaries illustrations, visit her website, ruthsanderson.com.

Get the dog's side of the story.

Sparky the fire dog is so good at her job that she knows when the alarm is going to ring *before* it even rings! But today is no ordinary day. There's no choice but to put Cinders—a rescue horse with an attitude—to work. But Cinders's very first fire is destined to become one of the greatest disasters of the nineteenth century!

DOG DIARIES

WALK A MILE IN THEIR PAWS.

EVERY DOG HAS A *TAIL* TO TELL.

RandomHouseKids.com

Collect all the books in the Horse Diaries series!

Elska

CATHERINE HAPKA

illustrated by RUTH SANDERSON

Bell's Star

ALISON HART

illustrated by RUTH SANDERSON

Koda

PATRICIA HERMES

illustrated by RUTH SANDERSON

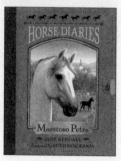

Maestoso Petra

JANE KENDALL

illustrated by RUTH SANDERSON

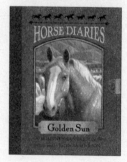

Golden Sun

illustrated by RUTH SANDERSON

Yatimah

CATHERINE HAPKA

illustrated by RUTH SANDERSON

HORSE DIARIES

Risky Chance

ALISON HART

illustrated by RUTH SANDERSON

HORSE DIARIES

Black Cloud

PATRICIA HERMES

HORSE DIARIES

Tennessee Rose

JANE KENDALL

HORSE DIARIES

Darcy

WHITNEY SANDERSON

illustrated by RUTH SANDERSON

HORSE DIARIES

Special Edition

Jingle Bells

CATHERINE HAPKA

illustrated by RUTH SANDERSON

HORSE DIARIES

Luna

CATHERINE HAPKA

illustrated by RUTH SANDERSON

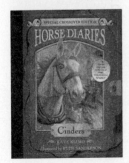

SPECIAL CROSSOVER EDITION

HORSE DIARIES

Cinders

KATE KLIMO

illustrated by RUTH SANDERSON

THE BLACK STALLION

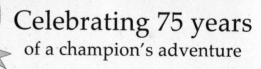